P9-CFG-064

STUFFER

STUFFER

WRITTEN AND ILLUSTRATED BY PETER PARNALL

Macmillan Publishing Company **New York**

Maxwell Macmillan Canada Toronto

Maxwell Macmillan International
New York Oxford Singapore Sydney

Macmillan Publishing Company is part of the Maxwell Communication Group of Companies.
Macmillan Publishing Company, 866 Third Avenue, New York, NY 10022.
Maxwell Macmillan Canada, Inc., 1200 Eglinton Avenue East, Suite 200, Don Mills, Ontario M3C 3N1.
First edition. Printed in Hong Kong

10 9 8 7 6 5 4 3 2 1

The text of this book is set in 14 pt. Baskerville. The illustrations are rendered in pencil and watercolor.

Library of Congress Cataloging-in-Publication Data. Parnall, Peter. Stuffer / written and illustrated by Peter Parnall. — 1st ed.   Summary: After being sold and mistreated, a pony eventually finds a happy home again. ISBN 0-02-770152-2   1. Ponies—Juvenile fiction. [1. Ponies—Fiction.] I. Title.
PZ10.3.P228St 1992   [Fic]—dc20   90-26997

In memory of
Stuffer

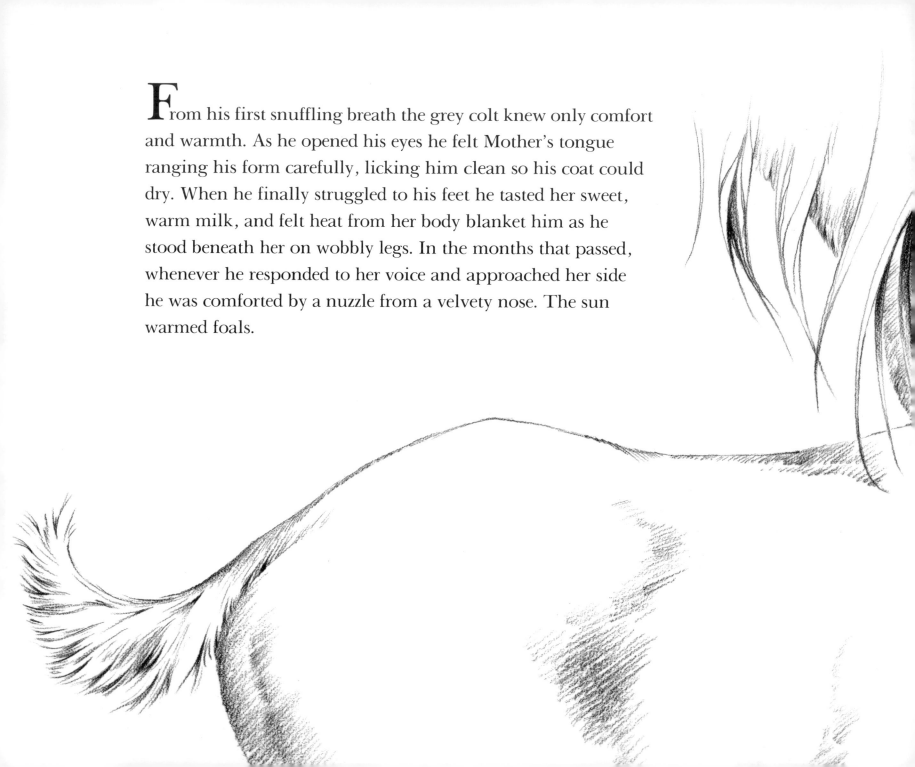

From his first snuffling breath the grey colt knew only comfort and warmth. As he opened his eyes he felt Mother's tongue ranging his form carefully, licking him clean so his coat could dry. When he finally struggled to his feet he tasted her sweet, warm milk, and felt heat from her body blanket him as he stood beneath her on wobbly legs. In the months that passed, whenever he responded to her voice and approached her side he was comforted by a nuzzle from a velvety nose. The sun warmed foals.

Butterflies, too.

Winter came: no comforting noses or nickers now. His playmates went to faraway homes. Only fences were left. High white fences that marked the snow. When his last friend headed toward a waiting truck the colt felt lost. With a burst of speed and a desperate leap he cleared the fence. Well, he got *over* the fence! Kind of.

He landed on the ground in a leggy heap. It did *not* go unnoticed. And what was "It"? Not his leap. Not the fact he was a pony on the loose. "It" was his courage.

This colt was special. He stayed at the farm, and on Christmas day a little girl found in her stocking a note which said, Look in the barn. She looked. In the corner of a stall was a giant red bow—with a pony attached. She named him Stocking Stuffer.

Girl. She wasn't very large—tiny, in fact. For the next two years she cared for Stuffer, teaching him about cats, dogs, and cows, and how good the ripe grapes were that grew behind the barn. Stuffer came when Girl called, and a good thing, too, for there wasn't a fence that could hold him now.

When he was five, everything changed. No more wandering and loafing with Girl; now there were lessons and jumps in a ring each day. Stuffer's training began, and some lonely set in as others took charge of his learning days. Girl was there, but beyond the fence. She came at night to give him treats. She brushed his face and whispered of summer sun, butterflies, and dark, ripe grapes.

Finally Stuffer and Girl were together again, jumping obstacles
in horse show rings. The jumps weren't as high as the fences
at home and together they won dozens of ribbons and bowls,
filling the tack room with silver and silk. Stuffer became
famous. Girl did too. But then she grew...and grew.

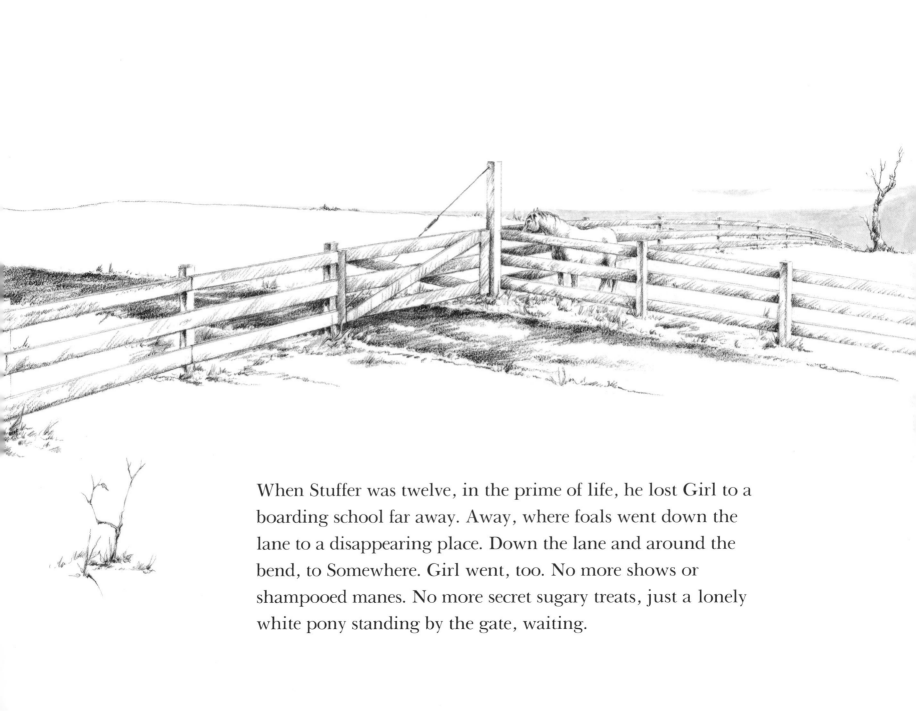

When Stuffer was twelve, in the prime of life, he lost Girl to a boarding school far away. Away, where foals went down the lane to a disappearing place. Down the lane and around the bend, to Somewhere. Girl went, too. No more shows or shampooed manes. No more secret sugary treats, just a lonely white pony standing by the gate, waiting.

"He's too small now," but Stuffer didn't hear. His ears shook with loud muffler sounds, and the smells of frightened horses filled his nose: smells of horses who had been hauled to places unknown in this, smelly, battered, rusty old van. Horses who never returned. Stuffer was frightened, as frightened as a pony could ever be. His world of white fences, sweet grass, and sun was replaced by darkness, loud noise, and choking fumes as the truck trundled off toward... Away.

He was unloaded at a stable as run-down as the truck. Thin horses peered from the darkness within and as he passed their stalls they snatched at him cruelly with long yellow teeth. He was put in a stall with a soggy floor.

Where was the sun?

For the next few years Stuffer was ridden far too hard. Ridden by people too big and too mean. His back ached, his feet ached, and his legs were on fire. Ribs stuck out like rails on a fence, for he was fed too little and used too much. His heart ached, too. A day arrived when his legs hurt so much, he could not rise from his reeking bed.

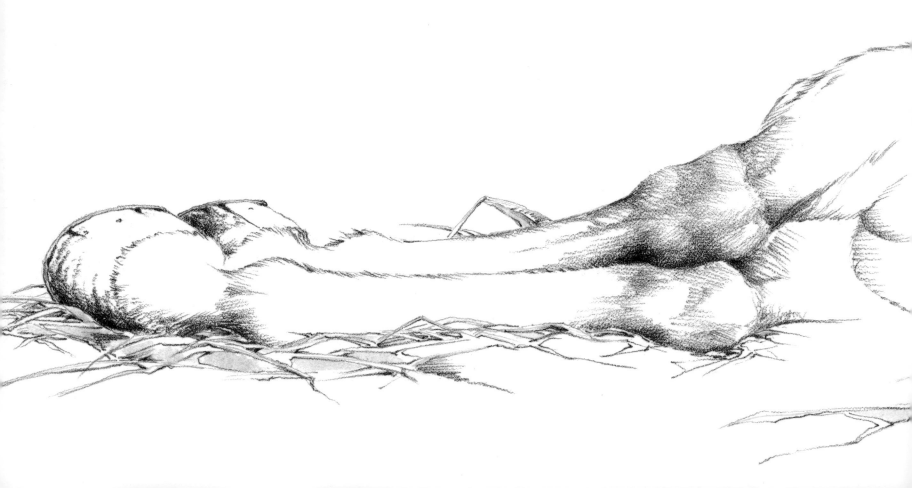

Other horses had left the stable crippled and worn, never to return. It was Stuffer's turn. He was dragged to a truck and taken away, unloaded at a barn more foul than before. He met animals like himself, too crippled or sick to fight or complain. On the night of the auction his turn finally came. He was led through the doors of the bidding ring, a tired old pony on painful legs. Above the murmur of the crowd a young voice cried out, "Daddy!" The searing lights blinded his eyes but his heart jumped when he heard that little girl sound. A moment later he hung his head in pain once more and was led back, back into darkness.

The next morning Stuffer was in a van again. This one was
clean, and there was green, sweet hay hanging from the wall in
a net by his head. His fear was overcome by the burning in his
legs and the taste in his mouth as he chewed the fresh smelling
hay,...slowly. Finally the truck slowed and through a window
by his head he saw clean, white fences. Everywhere. And grass....

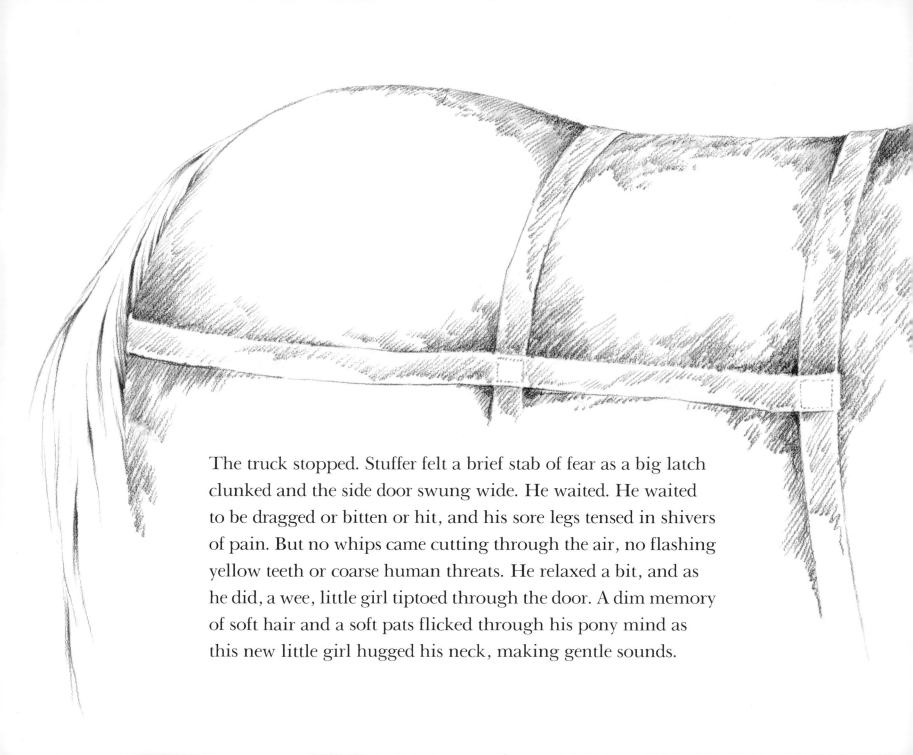

The truck stopped. Stuffer felt a brief stab of fear as a big latch clunked and the side door swung wide. He waited. He waited to be dragged or bitten or hit, and his sore legs tensed in shivers of pain. But no whips came cutting through the air, no flashing yellow teeth or coarse human threats. He relaxed a bit, and as he did, a wee, little girl tiptoed through the door. A dim memory of soft hair and a soft pats flicked through his pony mind as this new little girl hugged his neck, making gentle sounds.

Stuffer remembered gentle sounds.

And he remembered dark, ripe grapes...and butterflies.